Little Grey Rabbit

How Little Grey Rabbit Got Back Her Tail

Little Grey Rabbit

HOW LITTLE GREY RABBIT
GOT BACK HER TAIL

By Alison Uttley
Pictures by Margaret Tempest

templar
books

One cold morning, Little Grey Rabbit awoke at dawn, for this was to be a busy day.

Outside, she looked back at her little house and waved a paw to her sleeping friends, Hare and Squirrel. Then she scampered down the lane, swinging her basket over her head.

She was going to pick primroses for primrose wine. Hare had a bad cold and it is a certain cure.

As she walked, a black nose and two pink hands poked up in front of her.

"Hello," said Moldy Warp the Mole. "But where has your tail gone?"

"I gave it to Wise Owl," replied Grey Rabbit, "so that he would tell me where to get carrot seed."

"Oh, but wouldn't you like your tail back?" said Moldy Warp.

"Very, very much," answered Grey Rabbit sadly.

"I'll help you," said Mole. "I will think out a plan."

Back at the little house, Squirrel and Hare couldn't find Little Grey Rabbit anywhere. Hare ran up and down stairs with his head in a handkerchief, calling, "Where are you? A-tishoo! Are you hiding?"

Sneezing violently, he swept up the tablecloth and wrapped it round his shoulders.

Just then, there was a 'rat-a-tat-tat' at the door. It was Hedgehog with the milk. And right behind him was Grey Rabbit.

"Good morning," she said. "Look at my primroses. Now we can make primrose wine to cure Hare's cold!"

All day long they made the wine. Grey Rabbit packed the primroses in a wooden cask, added honey and wood-sorrell juice, then sealed it with beeswax.

"When can we have some?" asked Hare.

"In twenty-four hours," said Rabbit, and Hare began counting the minutes.

That night, Wise Owl flew over the house.

"Too-whit, a-tishoo! Too-whoo," he cried.

"Poor Wise Owl," murmured Grey Rabbit. "He has a cold too. I must take him some primrose wine."

But for now, all they could do was wait.

The next day, Robin brought
a letter saying 'Found Knock
Mole'. Nobody knew what it
meant, but they forgot all about
it when the wine was opened.

They filled their glasses.
Then Little Grey Rabbit
filled a bottle for Wise
Owl and set off into the
dark of the woods.

"I've brought some primrose wine," she called out.

"Thank you," said Owl. "What would you like in return?"

Little Grey Rabbit looked at her tail.

"Not that," said Owl. "Not unless you bring me another bell. But here is a book."

Grey Rabbit ran home with her book in her paws.

Moldy Warp was waiting for her, holding out a silver penny. "I thought it would do for Wise Owl's knocker," he said.

"How kind," said Rabbit. "But Owl will only give me back my tail in exchange for a bell."

"There's a bell in the village shop!" said Squirrel.

"Or there are bluebells in the woods," said Hare.

"I might make a bell," said Mole and he walked slowly out of the house.

After breakfast the next day, Squirrel put on her very best dress, and ran to the village shop.

'Tinkle, tinkle' went the bell as she darted inside. She leaped up onto the bell and it jangled loudly.

"Stop!" cried the shopkeeper. But Squirrel bit and tugged and pushed until the bell fell to the floor.

She picked it up and ran out of the door. But when she dragged it to Wise Owl, he shouted, "How can I sleep with that jingle-jangle? Take it away!"

Back home, Moldy Warp had made a little bell out of the old coin. When he shook it, a sweet silvery tinkle came from it.

So at dusk Grey
Rabbit started off to
see Wise Owl.

   "I've brought a bell
for my tail," she said
boldly.

Owl climbed down to admire it.
He hung the bell on his door and gave Grey
Rabbit her tail in exchange, stitching it on.
And by the time Little Grey Rabbit reached
home again, her tail was as good as ever.

THE END

A TEMPLAR BOOK

This edition first published in the UK in 2018 by Templar Publishing,
an imprint of Kings Road Publishing, part of the Bonnier Publishing Group,
The Plaza, 535 King's Road, London, SW10 0SZ
www.bonnierpublishing.com

Original edition first published in the UK in 1930
by William Collins Sons & Co Ltd

This edition edited by Susan Dickinson and Ruth Symons
Additional design by Nathalie Eyraud and Adam Allori

1 3 5 7 9 10 8 6 4 2

ISBN 978-1-78741-227-9

Printed in China